100+ Knock Knock Jokes for Kids

Johnny B. Laughing

"The Joke King"

ISBN: 1512279641
ISBN-13: 978-1512279641

DEDICATION

This book is dedicated to all the kids in the world that love knock knock jokes! Keep on laughing.

KNOCK KNOCK JOKES

Knock knock!
Who's there?
Four!
Four who?
Four he is a jolly good fellow!

Knock knock!
Who's there?
It's Sam!
It's Sam who?
It's Sam person that knocked on the door earlier!

Knock knock!
Who's there?
Butch!
Butch who?
Butch your arms around me!

Knock knock!
Who's there?
Two!
Two who?
Two be or not two be? That is the question.

Knock knock!
Who's there?
Jade!
Jade who?
Jade an entire birthday cake this morning!

Knock knock!
Who's there?
Ten!
Ten who?
Ten to your own business!

Knock knock!
Who's there?
Cassie!
Cassie who?
Cassie the forest for all the trees!

Knock knock!
Who's there?
Jess!
Jess who?
Jess the way it is!

Knock knock!
Who's there?
Bones!
Bones who?
Bones upon a time!

Knock knock!
Who's there?
Czech!
Czech who?
Czech before you open the door!

Knock knock!
Who's there?
Egg!
Egg who?
It's eggstremely cold out here. Open up!

Knock knock!
Who's there?
Tuna!
Tuna who?
Tuna guitar and it will sound much better!

Knock knock!
Who's there?
Bruce!
Bruce who?
I Bruce very easily. Please don't hit me!

Knock knock!
Who's there?
Sarah!
Sarah who?
Sarah other way in?

Knock knock!
Who's there?
Castro!
Castro who?
Castro bread upon the waters!

Knock knock!
Who's there?
Beef!
Beef who?
Beef fair now!

Knock knock!
Who's there?
Bruno!
Bruno who?
Bruno more tea for me!

Knock knock!
Who's there?
Ben Hur!
Ben Hur who?
Ben Hur an hour knocking on this door!

Knock knock!
Who's there?
Brie!
Brie who?
Brie me my supper!

Knock knock!
Who's there?
Bridget!
Bridget who?
London Bridget falling down, falling down!

Knock knock!
Who's there?
Candace!
Candace who?
Candace with love!

Knock knock!
Who's there?
Boiler!
Boiler who?
Boiler egg for 3-4 minutes!

Knock knock!
Who's there!
Bond!
Bond who?
Bond to succeed!

Knock knock!
Who's there?
Boise!
Boise who?
Boise ivy!

Knock knock!
Who's there?
Bun!
Bun who?
Bun-nies make great pets!

Knock knock!
Who's there?
Read!
Read who?
Read between the lines!

Knock knock!
Who's there?
Be!
Be who?
Because I'm worth it!

Knock knock!
Who's there?
Danielle!
Danielle who?
Danielle so loud! I heard you the first time!

Knock knock!
Who's there?
Becca!
Becca who?
Becca the net!

Knock knock!
Who's there?
Artichoke!
Artichoke who!
Artichoke when he ate too fast!

Knock knock!
Who's there?
Fido!
Fido who?
Fido I have to wait so long for you to open the door?

Knock knock!
Who's there?
Beaver E.!
Beaver E. who?
Beaver E. quiet and nobody will hear us!

Knock knock!
Who's there?
Attila!
Attila who?
Attila you no lies!

Knock knock!
Who's there?
Cannelloni!
Cannelloni who?
Cannelloni some money until next week?

Knock knock!
Who's there?
Cain!
Cain who?
Cain you tell? It's me!

Knock knock!
Who's there?
Byron!
Byron who?
Byron some new clothes!

Knock knock!
Who's there?
Callas!
Callas who?
Callas should be removed by a foot doctor!

Knock knock!
Who's there?
Buster!
Buster who?
Buster tire, can I use your phone?

Knock knock!
Who's there?
China!
China who?
China late, isn't it?

Knock knock!
Who's there?
Cameron!
Cameron who?
Cameron film are needed to take pictures!

Knock knock!
Who's there?
Ear!
Ear who?
Ear you are. I've been looking for you!

Knock knock!
Who's there?
Earl!
Earl who?
Earl be glad when you finally open the door!

Knock knock!
Who's there?
Bunny!
Bunny who?
The bunny thing is that I've forgotten now!

Knock knock!
Who's there?
Rain!
Rain who?
Rain deer. The same ones that lead Santa's sleigh.

Knock knock!
Who's there?
Twig!
Twig who?
Twig or tweat!

Knock knock!
Who's there?
Geno!
Geno who?
Geno any good jokes?

Knock knock!
Who's there?
Bing!
Bing who?
Bing down the house!

Knock knock!
Who's there?
Biafraid!
Biafraid who?
Biafraid, be very afraid!

Knock knock!
Who's there?
Bertha!
Bertha who?
Bertha-day wishes!

Knock knock!
Who's there?
Nadia!
Nadia who?
Nadia head while the music plays!

Knock knock!
Who's there?
Avery!
Avery who?
Avery time I come to your house we go through this!

Knock knock!
Who's there?
B-4!
B-4 who?
B-4 I freeze to death, please open this door!

Knock knock!
Who's there?
Carrie!
Carrie who?
Carrie me home, I'm tired!

Knock knock!
Who's there?
Ayatollah!
Ayatollah who?
Ayatollah you already!

Knock knock!
Who's there?
Biro!
Biro who?
Biro light of the moon!

Knock knock!
Who's there?
Edwin!
Edwin who?
Edwin some and you lose some!

Knock knock!
Who's there?
Shelby!
Shelby who?
Shelby coming around the mountain when she comes!

Knock knock!
Who's there?
Zany!
Zany who?
Zany one home? Open up!

Knock knock!
Who's there?
Bison!
Bison who?
Bison girl scout cookies!

Knock knock!
Who's there?
Bargain!
Bargain who?
Bargain up the wrong tree buddy!

Knock knock!
Who's there?
Paris!
Paris who?
Paris good but my favorite fruit is a peach!

Knock knock!
Who's there?
Beets!
Beets who?
Beets me, but I just forgot the joke!

Knock knock!
Who's there?
Basket!
Basket who?
Basket home, it's nearly dark!

Knock knock!
Who's there?
Comic!
Comic who?
Comic and see me anytime you want!

Knock knock!
Who's there?
Begonia!
Begonia who?
Begonia bother me!

Knock knock!
Who's there?
Bark!
Bark who?
Bark your car in the garage!

Knock knock!
Who's there?
Carl!
Carl who?
Carl get you there faster than walking will!

Knock knock!
Who's there?
Costa!
Costa who?
Costa bunch of money!

Knock knock!
Who's there?
Billy Braggs!
Billy Braggs who?
Billy Braggs too much. Tell him to stop!

Knock knock!
Who's there?
Bully!
Bully who?
Bully Jean is not my lover!

Knock knock!
Who's there?
Cantaloupe!
Cantaloupe who?
Cantaloupe with you tonight!

Knock knock!
Who's there?
Bellows!
Bellows who?
Bellows me some money! Can I have it please?

Knock knock!
Who's there?
Zeke!
Zeke who?
Zeke and ye shall find!

Knock knock!
Who's there?
Pain!
Pain who?
Pain in the neck!

Knock knock!
Who's there?
Bar-B-Q!
Bar-B-Q who?
Bar-B-Q, but I think you're even cuter!

Knock knock!
Who's there?
Adolf!
Adolf who?
Adolf ball hit me in the back!

Knock knock!
Who's there?
Bush!
Bush who?
Bush your money where your mouth is!

Knock knock!
Who's there?
Burton!
Burton who?
Burton in the hand is worth two in the bush!

Knock knock!
Who's there?
Bullet!
Bullet who?
Bullet all the hay and now he's hungry again!

Knock knock!
Who's there?
Cherry!
Cherry who?
Cherry oh, see you later!

Knock knock!
Who's there?
Bera!
Bera who?
Bera necessities!

Knock knock!
Who's there?
Census!
Census who?
Census lots of presents for Christmas!

Knock knock!
Who's there?
Bless!
Bless who?
I didn't sneeze!

Knock knock!
Who's there?
Scold!
Scold who?
Scold out here. Let me in!

Knock knock!
Who's there?
Caroline!
Caroline who?
Caroline of rope with you!

Knock knock!
Who's there?
Cartoon!
Cartoon who?
Cartoon up just fine. She purrs just like a cat!

Knock knock!
Who's there?
Camilla!
Camilla who?
Camilla minute!

Knock knock!
Who's there?
Razor!
Razor who?
Razor hands, this is a stick-up!

Knock knock!
Who's there?
Gluck!
Gluck who?
Gluck for a spare key for me to have!

Knock knock!
Who's there?
Bjorn!
Bjorn who?
Bjorn with a silver spoon in his mouth!

Knock knock!
Who's there?
Clarke!
Clarke who?
Clarke your car in the garage!

Knock knock!
Who's there?
Barry!
Barry who?
Barry the dead!

Knock knock!
Who's there?
Baron!
Baron who?
Baron mind who you're talking to!

Knock knock!
Who's there?
Fangs!
Fangs who?
Fangs for letting me in the house!

Knock knock!
Who's there?
Bat!
Bat who?
Bat you'll never guess!

Knock knock!
Who's there?
Arnie!
Arnie who!
Arnie having fun?

Knock knock!
Who's there?
Beggar!
Beggar who?
Beggar you don't know!

Knock knock!
Who's there?
Betty-Lou!
Betty-Lou who?
Betty-Lou a few pounds!

Knock knock!
Who's there?
Bashful!
Bashful who?
I can't tell you! I'm so embarrassed!

Knock knock!
Who's there?
Baby Owl!
Baby Owl who?
Baby Owl see you later, but maybe I won't!

Knock knock!
Who's there?
Bert!
Bert who?
Bert the dinner!

Knock knock!
Who's there?
Athena!
Athena who?
Athena reindeer landing on your roof!

Knock knock!
Who's there?
Beck!
Beck who?
Beckfast of champions!

Knock knock!
Who's there?
Wafer!
Wafer who?
Wafer a long time, but now I'm back!

Knock knock!
Who's there?
Auntie!
Auntie who?
Auntie glad to see me again!

Knock knock!
Who's there?
Fido!
Fido who?
Fido I have to wait so long for you to open the door?

ABOUT THE AUTHOR

The Joke King, Johnny B. Laughing is a best-selling children's joke book author. He is a jokester at heart and enjoys a good laugh, pulling pranks on his friends, and telling funny and hilarious jokes!

For more funny joke books just search for *JOHNNY B. LAUGHING* on Amazon.com

Visit the website:
www.funny-jokes-online.weebly.com

CPSIA information can be obtained at www.ICGtesting.com
Printed in the USA
LVOW06s1530131215

466484LV00001B/15/P